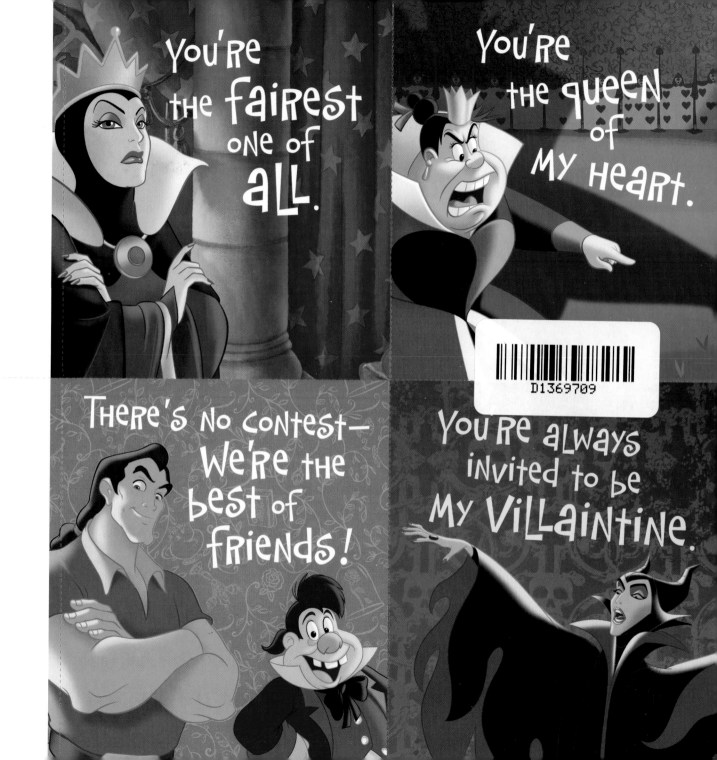

Happy Villaintine's Day

To: ____________________

From: ____________________

Happy Villaintine's Day

To: ____________________

From: ____________________

© Disney

Happy Villaintine's Day

To: ____________________

From: ____________________

© Disney

Happy Villaintine's Day

To: ____________________

From: ____________________

© Disney

Disney
VILLAINS
WILL YOU BE MY
Villaintine?

Manufactured in the United States of America

First Paperback Edition, December 2020

1 3 5 7 9 10 8 6 4 2

ISBN 978-1-368-06596-2

FAC-029261-20290
Library of Congress Control Number: 2020937026

For more Disney Press fun,
visit www.disneybooks.com

Roses are red.
Violets are blue.
Villains don't like love.
What's a sidekick
to do?

Sugar is sweet.
Villains can be tart.
Could sending
some Villaintines
help reach their hearts?

To: Ursula

From: Flotsam and Jetsam

Our feelings for you aren't fishy.

We're no poor unfortunate souls.

We're a match mermaid in heaven!

Being your poopsies never gets old.

There once was a man named Jafar, whom some would call strange and bizarre. But I'm his wingman forever. We're two birds of a feather. His scheming will take us both far!

Forget the jack,
the king, and the ace.
We only have eyes for you,
Your Grace.
You're even dazzling when
you're bright red.
For you, who wouldn't lose
their head?

To:
Cruella

From:
Horace
and
Jasper

To:
Scar

From:
Shenzi, Banzai,
and Ed

We're not wild about lions,
but we dislike you the least.
It's so fun to work with
a dark, scheming beast.
We're prepared to help you
with any little thing.
Just don't forget to bring us snacks.
Long live the king!

For you I'd walk the plank,
dear Hook,
leave a pirate's life for the land,
or sail the seas till the
end of time—
anything to give you a hand!

To: The Queen

From: Magic Mirror

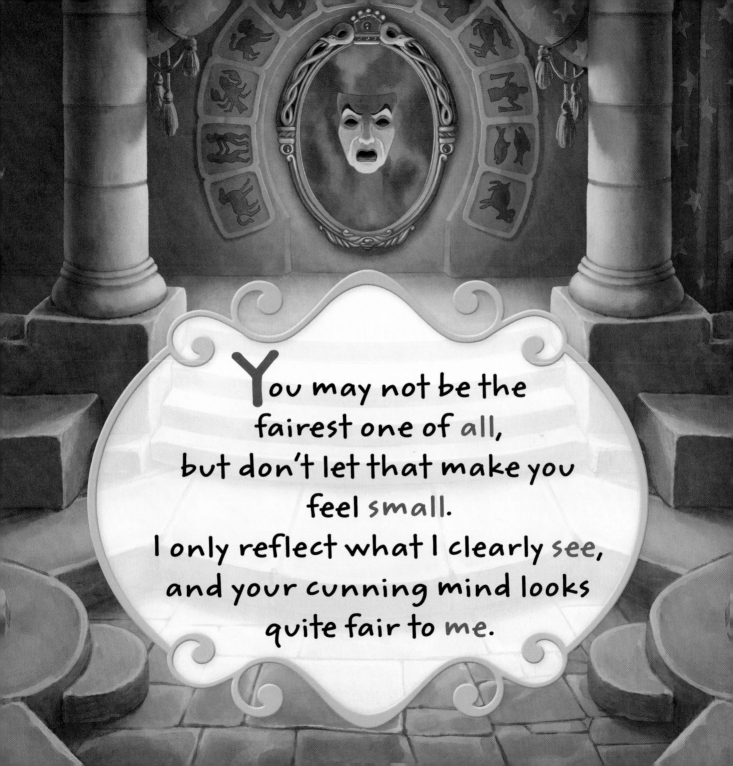

You may not be the fairest one of all, but don't let that make you feel small.
I only reflect what I clearly see, and your cunning mind looks quite fair to me.

To:
Maleficent

From:
The Raven

Greetings from your pet.
I have an invitation.
Forget about the royals
for a better situation.
Instead, let's laugh together
in our own private lair.
Not a thing can beat us
when we join forces to scare!

Of all your friends on
the other side,
you know I'm your
perfect match.
I don't have to ask if
you'll be mine.
We're already quite
attached!

To:
Gaston
From:
LeFou

No one's a friend like Gaston, perfect ten like Gaston, brings my lonely days to an end like Gaston.

His heart is as strong as an ox's.

There's no better guy than Gaston!

So even if a villain says,
"Love stinks!" "Ew, gross!"
"No way!"
their sidekicks know
they really do like
the joys of
Villaintine's Day.